Adrika Mukherjee

Funny Poems - A Collection by a Fourth Grader

Bumblebee Books
London

BUMBLEBEE PAPERBACK EDITION

Copyright © Adrika Mukherjee 2024

The right of Adrika Mukherjee to be identified as author of this work has been asserted in accordance with sections 77 and 78 of the Copyright, Designs and Patents Act 1988.

All Rights Reserved

No reproduction, copy or transmission of this publication may be made without written permission.
No paragraph of this publication may be reproduced, copied or transmitted save with the written permission of the publisher, or in accordance with the provisions of the Copyright Act 1956 (as amended).

Any person who commits any unauthorised act in relation to this publication may be liable to criminal prosecution and civil claims for damage.

A CIP catalogue record for this title is available from the British Library.

ISBN: 978-1-78796-073-2

Bumblebee Books is an imprint of
Olympia Publishers.

First Published in 2024

Bumblebee Books
Tallis House
2 Tallis Street
London
EC4Y 0AB

Printed in Great Britain
www.olympiapublishers.com

Inspector

Inspector Hector scanned the room,
He sniffed at every inch,
He peered at all the forks and spoons
The other things, he pinched.
He was suspicious of the drawing board,
And suspicious of the pencils.
I was getting very bored
When he looked at all my stencils.
He poked and prodded both my dogs,
And used a microscope for the car.
He even sniffed the leaves and logs,
And looked at every chocolate bar.
He licked at the table salt,
And sneezed on the pepper.
I'm getting very, very sick
Of that annoying Hector.
He put his nose in both my shoes
And climbed up all the trees,
And I was *so very mad*
when he started inspecting me!

Box

I'm trapped here,
In the box
And can't seem to get out.
I'm not smart
Like a fox
And not as strong
As an ox,
So, no wonder I'm trapped in here.
For everything
That passes me,
I hear a word or two,
And maybe, if I look real hard,
I see glimpses of their shoe.
It's so hot
In the box,
And I'm feeling rather sick
I think I have the chicken pox
And a couple ticks.
I hear the barking of a dog,
And the dripping of a spout,
--but I'm trapped in here,
and it's cramped in here,
so, my hearing's not so stout.
I'm trapped here,

In the box,
And no matter how I pout,
I'm still here,
In the box…
Oh, please get me out!

The Young Player of the Kazoo

You have angered me yet again,
Young player of the kazoo.
Your notes sound like squawking hens,
And your words are gibberish, too.
You have some mental issues,
And have a tend to sneeze
You've used up all my tissues,
Stop bothering me, please!
Young player of the kazoo,
You anger me so!
Especially because
You're a good-for-nothing crow!

Etcetera

So pretty are you, under this light
So smart are you, with a mind so bright
So academic are you, with a mathematical mind
So sweetly you smile when I look through your eyes
So honest are you, empty of lies
So pretty are you, under this light
With a heart full of cares
And a mind full of rights.

Sleep

I'm very, very tired
But can't seem to fall asleep.
I've closed my eyes one thousand times
And counted every sheep.
I've stared at the ceiling
And rolled and rolled around
I even put on headphones
To block out any sound.
I've thought of lots of things,
Like which home to retire in,
But when I finally fell asleep,
I slept through the tornado siren!

Goldilocks

Let me tell you the story
Of *Goldilocks and Three Bears*.
I edited it a bit, but not too much, I swear!
Goldilocks found their hut
With bushes finely cut
While the bears were away
On their small holiday.
She ate up all their supper
And slept in all their beds,
And when the bears came home,
She jumped on all their heads.
Then Goldilocks flew away
with her jetpack of the day.
That is the story of Goldilocks.
I edited it a bit
And it took a lot of time,
So, I hoped you liked it!

The Purple Purse

I have a purple purse
That everyone stays away from,
Because it has a curse,
To question it is dumb.
It hides a couple ghosts
And hundreds of scary creatures,
But what it hides the most
Are terrifying, tortured teachers.
It's full of rampaging monsters,
And screaming in the halls,
There's an evil lobster
In every bathroom stall.
You also shouldn't go near
The potions that mix and collide.
Still, come check out my purple purse!
Come on, don't be shy!
But, if you get too close,
You might have to go inside.

Dogs and Cats

Is the dog different from the cat?
Yes? I don't know about that.
On a chair my dog has sat
And you know what? So did my cat!
My cat just went inside a log
And you know what? So did my dog!
My cat can catch a ball!
My dog cuddles in cold winter and fall!
Cats aren't lazy.
Dogs aren't chasy.
The connection's quite hazy,
But it's not *that* hard to see
If you're a smart person like me.

The Door

When I open my door,
I see my bedroom floor
And then I close it and open it again.
This time I see
A tall walnut tree
And I shut it and open it again.
And there's Cinderella,
Holding her umbrella,
And I close it and open it again.
And there's Sherlock Holmes,
Dressed in big shoes,
Looking around for helpful clues,
And I shut it and open it again,
And this time I see, yet again,
My wonderful bedroom floor.

The Dog Era

You'll have seen them in your house,
For when the Dog Era came
For all the dog haters,
Oh, what a shame.
Dogs of all sizes,
Of all shapes and colors,
Instead of trophy prizes,
Golden dog collars.
Adoptions were closed
Because there's tons of dogs out there,
The fashion-dogs posed,
And the brave-dogs gave dares.
The laundromat was a sleeping place for dogs,
And the playground was even more of a hog!
But then I woke up!
The Dog Era was a dream.
I looked around-
Not a dog to be seen!

Hello, Vacation

It's summer break
Hello, vacation!
We're going to California
And we're at the train station.
I want to take my dog.
He's sweet and adorable,
But he's not allowed,
And I don't think he's portable.
I want to take our smaller dog.
Pretty, pretty please?
But the hotel owner is allergic.
Says they make him sneeze.
It's winter break
Hello, vacation!
We're off to Mexico
And we're at the ferry station.
I want to take the piano.
It's the only instrument I play.
But it's way, way too big!
Maybe another day.
I want to take the guitar.
I can learn it while we're there,
But there isn't any space.
No suitcases to share.

It's spring break
Hello, vacation!
We're heading to Rome
And we're at the plane station.
I want to take the dictionary
In case I hear any new words,
But it's seriously too heavy.
It's either the dictionary or the smores.
I want to take my notepad
So I can write everything down,
But mom says I can't take it!
Now *that* made me frown.
It's autumn break
Hello, vacation!
We're aiming for San Diego
And we're at the taxi station.
I want to take the aloe vera
So I can have aloe vera juice,
But Mom disagrees.
She thinks the soil will get loose.
I want to take the venus flytrap
Any bug it eats will die!
But Mom says I don't need to
because there aren't any flies.
Hello, vacation!
Let's have a good time.
I'm here for a staycation
And a couple rhymes.

Evergreen

Bright tree with dark leaves,
Tall as the sky,
How did you get there?
Surely you can't fly.
Dark tree with bright leaves,
Sucking up the sun,
Your leaves don't run away
When winter comes.
Bright tree with bright leaves,
You are tall and lean,
Forever, forever, for evergreen.

Desert Sound

The sound of the desert is crystal clear.
You'll hear it soon enough—just use your ears!
Just ignore the groan of the camels
And the flip-flapping flannel
And the slide of golden sand
And the heavy metal band
And the happy and the sorrow
And the talking of tomorrow
Ignore the barking of that dog
Ignore the rustling leaves and logs
Ignore the pyramids, so great and tall
(They look like they're about to fall!)
But if you ignore all this noise, you see,
You'll hear the desert --- trust me!

Lilypad

I saw a little swimming thing
When I was by the river;
I was lucky to have seen it,
For it showed by just a sliver.
A cheery little thing it was,
A green so fresh and pure;
Floating in the waters deep,
A beauty to endure.
A little pad, just floating there,
As night shined overhead,
And its beauty continued to shine
As the city went to bed.
Something that no one noticed,
Something behind-the-scenes,
Something that was so beautiful
That no one seemed to see.
I watched the little floating pad
All throughout the night;
I followed it through every current,
Never letting it out of sight.
Then finally, when dawn erupted
Across the once-lifeless sky,
I decided to give the thing a name
Before I said goodbye.

A thing that was so beautiful,
So bright, so fresh and calm,
It was a thing simply divine,
Like a bluebird's song.
I finally decided on what
To call the thing;
The name was just so nice
That it made me want to sing.
The thing was so awfully pretty,
A calm and floating pad,
It was like a little lily,
A little Lilypad.

The Dog's Adventure
(Based on a true story)

There once was a labradoodle
Who went into the oceans deep,
It started in the car,
Where she sat in the backseat.
They were driving by the sea,
Where the water was filled with ships,
And the dog, so awfully bored,
Wanted to take a dip.
But she knew her owners wouldn't let her,
So, she leapt out of the seat
Out through the open window,
And landed on her feet.
She climbed down to the beach,
With her family shouting far behind,
And jumped into the sea
Into the waters, clear and pristine.
She swam a couple miles,
And saw different kinds of coral,
But then a fisherman fished her up,
And started a big quarrel.
The crew looked at her collar,
In which a phone number was inscribed,
And the captain said into the speaker,

"We have your dog inside!"
And so, the puppy was sent home,
But there was something in her mouth.
Her owners bent down to see what it was-
-a simply enormous trout!!!

Professor Piano

He was good in science
And English and math;
He'd written ten books on
the science of bath,
It was said that he, the professor,
Could do anything,
From studies to chores
To engineering.
One day, he was walking
Across the street,
When he met a young pianist,
Who sat at his feet,
And she said,
"I think I can do more things than you."
The professor snapped back,
"There is nothing *I* cannot do!"
The pianist, she smirked,
and folded her hands.
"I suppose, then, you have played in a band?"
The professor didn't want to admit
That he hadn't done such a thing,
So, he said with great charm, to the pianist's alarm,
"I can play the piano and sing."
The pianist took him by the arm

And pulled him along, up to the top of the sidewalk,
"The music contests right there.
You should win fair and square, if you truly believe in such talk."
The professor, he nodded,
And bravely walked up.
The pianist was excited
To see him give up.
Inside the room was quiet,
So everyone could hear.
The professor walked up,
Trembling with fear.
He sat on the bench
In a bad starting position,
And played the first note
Of a bad composition.
But he was so scared
That he ran quite away;
Everyone heard him,
For he screamed the whole way.

So It Was

I met a mathematician once
With a truly empowered brain.
She could solve all my problems
Without a bit of strain.
I asked her how she'd harnessed
A power oh so great,
And she said that it all started
At her neighbor's front gate.
She was thinking very hard
About opening that door,
Thinking harder, harder,
And harder furthermore.
And if a simple door
Could bring thoughts so great,
She just *had* to go
And open up that gate.
I asked her, "Why?
Why did you open up that gate?"
And she said, "Just because."
So it was, so it was.
She'd told me her story,
Thus I'd have to tell mine.
She asked me so very nicely,
That I had to say it was fine.

It was a stormy night,
And I was missing my dog.
I was lost in the forest,
Scared alone in the fog.
Whilst running through the wood,
Past trees scarily tall,
What appeared before me
Was a crystal ball.
It brought me home quite safely,
And I gave happy laughter.
Then I stayed with my family
Happily ever after.
And she asked, "Why?
Why did you touch that crystal ball?"
And I said, "Just because."
So it was, so it was.

Two Dogs in a Bone

When my two dogs share a bone,
They're like two bubbles in a foam.
They're like sweet in sour in a toffee
Or the sugar and salt in a coffee.
You can say that I'm wrong,
And that it's really 'two peas in a pod',
But if you're describing *my* dogs,
It sounds kind of odd.
They're two houses in a home,
Two flavors in a cone.
They're two types of liquid in one cup,
They're two puppies in one pup.
But at the end of the day,
Needless to say,
They're really just my dogs.

The Scientist

Do not question the scientist.
He knows much more than you.
Do not question the scientist.
He knows a lot, it's true.
Do not question the scientist.
He's in a foul mood,
Because he's rather hungry,
And he ate up all his food.
Do not question the scientist.
It might sound silly to you,
But it's very, very, very, very, very, very true.

Bird

High in the sky,
A bird does fly,
Flapping its wings
To and fro.
And the people
Far below,
Gasp in awe
And watch it go,
For hypnotic beauty
The bird does show.
Higher and higher
The bird does go,
Flapping its wings
To and fro,
Until it's so high
Up in the sky
That the beautiful bird
Is out of sight.

Leaf

I watch a maple leaf blow
In the autumn wind,
Circling around a small
Group of kids.
I watch an old, shaggy leaf
Land on a nearby bird,
Who tossed it away
In an angry curve.
Then I saw a clean, green leaf
Float in front of a car driving near,
And when the car passed by,
The leaf disappeared.
Then my mom called me for dinner,
And my happiness got dimmer,
Because I wanted to watch more leaves crash into cars,
Not go inside and eat oatmeal bars.

Tail

I watch my dog's tail wag
And knock over some bags.
I watch the tail of my cat
As she chases a rat.
I watch the tail of my ferret
As she chews on a carrot.
I watch the tail of my bird
Sway in a happy curve,
And I wonder,
Why don't humans have tails, too?

Once Upon a Time

Once upon a time,
I came up with a rhyme,
But it wasn't really funny,
And really kind of crummy.
I watch this poem crumble
Into a room with ten other poets,
And one picks up this book,
And reads *Once Upon a Time*,
And then he tells me,
"You can really rhyme."

The Bark

My dog barks at midnight,
His tail wagging in the moonlight.
I say, "Be quiet!" but he ignores me
And takes off after a bird in a tree.
I chase him at the speed of a rocket,
As he rips a torch from my mother's torch socket.
His tail gets caught in the flame,
And he howls as loud as an incoming train.
This wakes up the neighbors,
And for not controlling my dog, they call me a traitor.
The neighbors chase me, and I chase my dog,
And he chases the bird, who takes a fast curve,
And me, my dog, and the neighbors all smash into a tree.
This all started with one bark, you see.

Soccer

I'm playing long, long soccer
I just need to play a little bit longer
It just gets harder and harder
Each time I kick the ball into the net.
I'm the captain of my team,
And no matter how easy soccer might seem,
It's the hardest sport *I've* ever seen------
Oops. The ball missed when I kicked.
The goalie caught it... I really wanted...
Another chance... I'm in a trance...
Now do you see how hard Soccer might be?

Foot-ball Football

I'm playing foot-ball football,
Which is crazy, all-in-all,
For every single one of us
Who goes after the ball.
My best friend Sophie
Just smashed into a tree,
And so did Natalie,
My number-one enemy.
So I'm the last one left, you see,
On my losing team,
They shout, "Get the ball, Lucy!"
But Coach blows his whistle
And they stop overestimating me.

Silent

I wonder why some people are so silent.
It's annoying when they're always quiet.
And when they *do* talk, It's really a shock
When their voice is as soft as a feather.
"I had to bend down to hear silent kids!"
says my second-grade teacher.
So as you can see, it would really be easier
If your voice wasn't a quiet mumble.
And if your voice *does* stumble
To that tone of a tumble,
Just apologize, is all!

Dream

A tiny spark of yellow
Yet rainbow in the sky,
I wish to see these colors
But now I wish to fly.
I would touch every single color,
And then I would know why.
Are they actually together, or could it be a lie?

I flew and flew and flew,
And then I said goodbye to the world of Black
And hello to the Blue.
And then I met, and then I met, and then I met you!
And then I had the thought if this could be a dream,
Or if this planet would explode,
Or if we would be seen by someone with a telescope
Who looked scary and mean.

So I said goodbye to you,
And to plant Blue,
Hello to planet Black,
And said, "Greetings! I'm back!".

When I Grow Up

I'll grow up to name the clouds,
And blow the wind,
And dry the grounds.
I'll grow up and turn stone to gold,
And tell stories till they're all told.

I'll pick out diamonds from the earth,
And stop people from crying at birth.
I'll turn bad things into stone,
And bring company to those who feel alone.
I'll pet the dogs and pet the cats,
And turn the weak into acrobats!
I'll teach the weak how to fly,
And teach the tough how to cry,
I'll weave a picture of us all,
And paint murals in every single hall.
I'll make us certain, make us wise,
And rid us of every cunning lie.
I'll make our lives as true,
And paint the skies so blue.
That far before I'm even done,
There's happiness in everyone.

I'll grow up to name the clouds,
And blow the wind,
And dry the grounds.
Yes, I'll erase every evil mark,
Far before the sky gets dark.

About the Author

Adrika Mukherjee is a fourth grader who enjoys writing, playing piano, tennis, and running with her two dogs. Adrika believes in access to education for all. She wants to donate all proceedings from the sale of the book to Seattle Children's Hospital. Adrika is an avid reader and writer who also tutors younger elementary kids in her school. Her favorite subject is astronomy. Adrika aspires to write scripts for movies someday, as well as compose music for the same. Adrika resides in Seattle, Washington with her parents and two dogs - Rosco and Zuri.

Acknowledgements

I want to thank my parents who always supported and encouraged me to read and write.